Play It Again

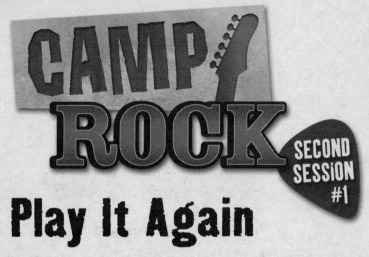

SECOND SESSiON #1

Play It Again

Adapted by Phoebe Appleton

Based on "Camp Rock," Written by Karin Gist & Regina Hicks and Julie Brown & Paul Brown

DISNEY PRESS

New York

Printed in the United States of America

First Edition
1 3 5 7 9 10 8 6 4 2

Library of Congress Catalog Card Number: 2008925711
ISBN 978-1-4231-1615-8

For more Disney Press fun, visit www.disneybooks.com
Visit DisneyChannel.com

CHAPTER ONE

Mitchie Torres opened her eyes. Sunlight streamed across her bed and birds chirped outside. A huge smile spread across her face. She had never thought in her wildest dreams that she would make it to Camp Rock. And now she was about to start Second Session! Pushing back the covers, Mitchie pinched her arm. Nope, definitely not a dream. She was still at the coolest camp in the world.

She had been convinced that as soon as Final Jam was over, she and her mom would be packing up Connie's Catering and heading home. But then Camp Rock's director, Brown Cesario, had asked Connie to stay on for another session. And that meant Mitchie got to stay, too! Starting today, she could look forward to more days of singing, dancing, and jamming with her new friends. Just thinking about it made her smile widen.

Caitlyn Gellar, Mitchie's best friend at camp, was sitting on her own bunk. The laptop she was almost never without was over her knees. "Geez," she said, catching sight of Mitchie's smile. "You haven't even gotten up yet and already you're on the right side of the bed!"

Mitchie stretched her arms over her head. "Of course I am! It's another day at Camp Rock!" As her sleepy eyes opened wider, she spotted the laptop. "What are you working on?" she asked.

"Check it out," Caitlyn said excitedly. She struck a key, and suddenly an energetic beat filled the cabin.

"That sounds great!" Mitchie exclaimed, her head bopping to the music.

Caitlyn smiled and then turned it off. "Thanks," she replied. "It's *so* cool we get to share the Beat Cabin this session. No more dealing with Tess Tyler and her entourage."

Mitchie nodded in agreement as she got out of bed. She pulled her long, brown hair into a ponytail. "I'll miss Ella and Peggy," Mitchie said, referring to her former cabin-mates. "But I'm okay with having some space from Tess. Even if she seemed nicer after Final Jam, I think it's going to take some more proof before I fully believe it."

Just speaking about Tess deflated Mitchie's good mood. But she quickly brushed that aside. This was a time for new beginnings.

"What kind of proof are you looking for?" Caitlyn asked. "I, for one, would like to see her save a child, feed the poor . . ." her voice trailed off.

Mitchie laughed. Caitlyn was never afraid to say what was on her mind—a skill Mitchie sometimes wished she had.

The sound of the door creaking open caused both girls to turn around. Brown was standing in the doorway wearing jeans and a Van Halen T-shirt. He looked like a total rocker— which he sort of was. He was one of the founding members of the band Wet Crows, and musical skill clearly ran in the family. His nephew, Shane Gray, was a huge pop star, not to mention a current guest instructor at Camp Rock—and Mitchie's friend.

"Still basking in the glow of that amazing Final Jam?" he asked after saying hello to both girls.

Mitchie and Caitlyn smiled. It still felt like a dream. After Tess had accused them of stealing her charm bracelet, Brown had banned them from any and all activities until the end of Final Jam—*the* event of the summer so far. Luckily, they had found a way to take the stage, and Mitchie had totally rocked out.

The whole camp had gotten wrapped up in her song—including Shane. It turned out that Mitchie was the girl he had been trying to find all summer. The girl with "the voice." When he realized it, he had jumped up on the stage and sang with her. It had been an amazing end—and a great beginning, too.

Mitchie hadn't won the jam, but it hadn't mattered. Being onstage, in front of everyone, singing her song and not being scared, had been totally amazing. Mitchie couldn't wait to do it again.

"You bet!" Caitlyn exclaimed. Her smile matched the one on Mitchie's face.

"Glad to hear it, mates. Now, I gotta run! Have to welcome the new campers and get all the events in order." Waving good-bye,

Brown walked out the door, letting it slam behind him. A moment later, the girls heard his feet clomping down the stairs.

"I wonder who the new kids are?" Mitchie asked. It would be fun to have fresh faces around, but she was glad that some familiar ones—Lola, Peggy, Andy, Barron, Sander, Ella, and even Tess—were back.

"I guess we'll find out," Caitlyn replied. "But before that, I was thinking—it would be cool to try and create our own sound before summer is over, you know? But it'll take some work."

"Sure thing," Mitchie said. She walked over to her dresser and grabbed a purple shirt and a denim skirt. Throwing them on, she quickly brushed her teeth and ran a comb through her hair.

"Have fun with Shane," Caitlyn said as Mitchie headed for the door.

Mitchie blushed. "How did you know I was going to see Shane?"

Caitlyn rolled her eyes. "I might always have my nose in this computer, but I'm not blind!"

"Could that be the former bad boy of Connect Three?" Mitchie asked, peeking her head around the edge of a hollowed-out tree trunk. Shane Gray was sitting on a nearby bench, waiting for her. They exchanged smiles as Mitchie sat down next to him.

"Hey, look, my label may have sent me here because of my bad-boy attitude," he joked, "but I am fully cured now!"

Shane had ended up at Camp Rock kind of by accident. After a minor freak-out at a video shoot, Shane's label—and his band-mates—had decided some good PR was in order. So they had packed him up and sent him to Camp Rock. They hoped a guest-instructor job would help him get his head on straight.

"Hmm . . ." Mitchie teased. "This fresh air must *really* work wonders."

Shane grinned. Mitchie was only half right. The camp was grounding, but it was more than that. It was Mitchie and her support that had really inspired him to change. He was about to say just that when a familiar voice rang out, ruining the moment.

Looking down the path, Mitchie and Shane caught sight of Tess sashaying toward them. As usual, she was a little overdressed for camp, in a glitter tunic and leggings. The pendant around her neck sparkled in the sun, and her gold charm bracelet twinkled as she walked.

"Shane! I've been looking all over for you," Tess said, giving Shane a wide smile. "Mitchie!" she added, a note of disappointment in her voice. "I thought you were going home."

"Nope," Mitchie said happily. "Brown liked Mom's cooking so much, we're staying!"

"That's great," Tess said insincerely. "I hope you won't have to spend all your time working in the kitchen." She smirked.

Mitchie took a deep breath. She knew Tess wasn't really mean. She could just be a little bit of a diva. It wasn't surprising. After all, her mom was an award-winning recording artist. To Tess, status was everything. To try and impress her, Mitchie had actually lied and pretended that she was someone she wasn't. When Tess found out the truth—that Mitchie was the daughter of the kitchen help—she had given her a hard time. But that was then. Now Mitchie was much more confident.

"I am still going to help my mom," Mitchie said with a smile. "But that doesn't mean I won't be giving my all to music. And . . ." she couldn't resist adding, ". . . to the next competition."

"Hey," Shane said, interrupting the two girls. "You were looking for me, Tess?"

Tess waved her hand in the air. "Oh, never mind," she said haughtily. "I'll tell you later." She shook her head and tossed her long, blonde hair over her shoulder. "I have to go. My mother is calling me from some party in the Hamptons. Wouldn't want to miss it."

Turning around, she headed back the way she had come, leaving Mitchie and Shane alone.

"So, what were you saying?" Mitchie asked shyly.

"Oh." Shane bit his lip. Tess had ruined the moment. "I was going to tell you that . . . uh, Nate is coming to visit," he finished, the lie floating off his tongue.

Mitchie grinned. Nate was part of Connect Three. She had met him at Final Jam and knew how much he meant to Shane. It would be good to have him around.

Mitchie glanced at her watch and let out a gasp. "Oh, no! I have to go!" she cried. "Kitchen duty calls. Sorry to bail. We'll talk later, okay?"

"Sure," Shane answered. "I really want you to listen to the song Peggy and I recorded," he told her. "I'd love to get your input."

Mitchie was thrilled. "Of course!" she exclaimed. "I'd do it now if I didn't have to work."

"You've got your responsibilities," Shane said, smiling. "Just don't forget!"

"I won't. I promise." Mitchie waved good-bye and took off down the path.

As Shane watched Mitchie run away, he shook his head. Sometimes I just don't get you, Shane, he said to himself. Fishing his cell phone out of his pocket, he dialed a number. "Hey, Nate," he said when his friend's voice mail picked up. "It's me. I hope you've got some free time coming up, because I kind of need you to get here. Like, right now."

CHAPTER TWO

"**H**ey, girls," Connie Torres said cheerfully as she walked into the kitchen that was attached to the Mess Hall of Fame. "Ready for more culinary adventures?"

Mitchie nodded as she tied on her apron. Beside her, Caitlyn did the same. Even though Caitlyn's kitchen duty was no longer mandatory, she still liked hanging out with Mitchie and her mom. It was relaxing in the kitchen. Plus, she had first access to the tasty treats Connie created.

"So, I want the first lunch of this session to be extraspecial," Connie said. "I was thinking turkey burgers and sweet-potato fries. Which means . . ."

"Sweet-potato peeling!" Mitchie and Caitlyn said in unison.

Connie laughed and placed two giant sacks of potatoes onto the stainless steel table. "One peels," she said, her eyes twinkling. "And one goes to the camp office to pick up some supply orders for me."

"You go," Caitlyn said, turning to Mitchie. "The sound of those industrial dishwashers chugging away is inspiring a great bass line."

Mitchie didn't need to be asked twice. She took off her apron and sailed out the door. All around her she could hear campers tuning guitars and practicing scales. She even heard the soft, cool sounds of a clarinet making its way through the treetops. Mitchie smiled. There was no place quite like Camp Rock. The clarinet sound filtered into her head and formed into a little tune. As she walked along, she hummed it happily.

Suddenly, a gruff, older man's voice broke through the peace. "Music is a hobby. There's no future in it," the voice snarled. Looking to her right, Mitchie saw that she was passing the visitors' parking lot. A yellow truck was idling in the lot. A tall boy she'd never seen before stood next to the truck's open door holding a duffel bag and a guitar. He had dark, wavy hair that was tucked carelessly under a faded red ball cap and a wiry build. Mitchie couldn't tell how tall he was because at the moment he was slumped over as he submitted to a scolding.

The man's voice was coming from the driver's side of the truck. "Spend what time you can here," he was saying. "I'm paying a small fortune and if I have even the slightest reason to come back and get you, I will."

Then the door slammed shut, and the truck drove away.

For a few moments, the boy just stood there, looking sadly in the direction of the disappearing truck. Watching, Mitchie couldn't help but wonder what was going on inside the boy's head. Suddenly, a line popped into her head: *You have secrets that you can't tell. Secrets for me and no one else.* It went along with the tune she had been humming before.

While she wanted to stay and see where the song went, Mitchie knew she had to get to the office. Taking a step back, a branch snapped underfoot. In the stillness of the woods, it sounded as loud as thunder.

The boy spun around, his eyes coming to rest on Mitchie.

"Oh," Mitchie said, feeling her cheeks flush. "Sorry! I wasn't spying on you. I was just walking by. And I saw you, and I didn't mean to stare at you, it's just that I got this idea for a song, and . . ." She put her hand over her mouth. "Sorry. Again."

The boy took off his hat and brushed a lock of hair off his forehead. Hoisting his duffel bag up on his shoulder, he looked resigned. "It's all right. I'll see you around." Then, before Mitchie could respond, he turned and headed down the path that led to the cabins.

"So, you want to tell me why I'm here?" Nate asked, shaking his head as he unpacked.

After getting Shane's message, he had gotten to Camp Rock as fast as he could. His friend had sounded pretty desperate—which was so *not* Shane. The hasty departure explained the T-shirt Nate now pulled out of his duffel. It was two sizes too small—*and* purple.

"It's a long story," Shane groaned. But it *shouldn't* be, he added silently. All I had to do was tell Mitchie what her support means to me. But did I do that? No. Instead, I chickened out and told her Nate was coming. Talk about smooth.

Nate looked over at his friend. "I'm a busy guy," he said, "but I always have time to hear about Shane and his crazy schemes. So I repeat—why am I here?"

Before Shane could explain, Brown and Dee La Duke, the camp's music director, appeared in the doorway. "Nate!" Dee cried. "This is a nice surprise."

Nate smiled. Dee and Brown were practically family. "Oh, I was just getting ready to take a few days off while Jason is hanging with some friends. And then I thought, where do I really want to be? Lying on a beach somewhere or back where we created our sound? It was a pretty easy decision." Laughing, he ran a hand through his curly brown hair.

Brown grinned. "Glad to have you back. It's going to be a great session. We'll see you guys in a few. Got to set up the first event!"

Nate placed his now-empty duffel bag under the bed. "I guess we better go, too. You can fill me in later," he said. Then he sighed. "If I expect to actually fall asleep on this bunk, I am going to have to work really hard every day."

"Hey, Nate," Shane said. "Thanks, man. I'm glad you're here."

Nate slapped him on the back. "Hey, that's what bandmates—and friends—are for."

CHAPTER THREE

When Mitchie and Caitlyn arrived at the mess hall for lunch, Peggy Dupree and Lola Scott were already eating. At the table next to them, Tess sat picking at her food. A girl with thick red hair, freckles, and an upturned nose was sitting next to Tess.

"That's Tess's new groupie," Caitlyn whispered to Mitchie as they sat down. Caitlyn prided herself on knowing the latest camp news before anyone else. "Her name is Lorraine Burgess. Apparently, she thinks the sun rises and sets on Tess."

Mitchie glanced over. Sure enough, Lorraine was bobbing her head as Tess talked—most likely about herself. Mitchie sighed. Not that long ago, she had been just like Lorraine. . . .

"Speaking of new kids," Lola said, giggling. "I think I might be in love!"

"I heard that he's a musical genius," Peggy commented. Obviously she knew who Lola was talking about. "There's something so intense about him."

"He has a Stratocaster. Did you see it?" Lola asked, twirling a lock of her curly hair around her finger.

Mitchie looked back and forth between her two friends. "Who are you talking about?" she asked in confusion.

Lola pointed across the room. Turning, Mitchie saw the boy from the parking lot. He was wearing the same faded ball cap, and Mitchie couldn't help but think he looked a little out of place. He should be playing sports or hanging out on a golf course, she thought. Then she stopped herself. Camp Rock was all about being the real you. She shouldn't judge.

Suddenly, the boy raised his head. His eyes met Mitchie's. He waved and rambled casually toward her table.

"Hey," he said, giving Mitchie a smile. "Sorry about earlier. I'm Colby Miller."

The whole table—except Caitlyn, who stayed focused on the laptop in front of her—stared at him. "I'm Mitchie," she said. "And these are . . ."

Tap, tap, tap. At the front of the mess hall, Brown was hitting the microphone with a butter knife. "Better get back to my seat," Colby said. "Catch ya later." Mitchie watched him walk over and sit down next to her friend Andy.

"First of all, I want to say welcome to all our new campers," Brown began. "Let's make sure we show them a good time!" The room filled with cheers and whoops. Brown let them go on for a moment and then waved his hands for quiet. "Now on to what I'm sure you are all eager to know—how we're going to start off this session. . . ."

More applause followed, and Andy banged out a drumroll on his table.

"The first thing we're going to do is . . . make music videos! You'll be split into two groups and are expected to come up with a song, create a video concept, and film it. Then, once we've seen the finished product, we will determine a winner."

The campers began to trade high fives. Caitlyn was grinning from ear to ear. This was the perfect activity for her! "I already have the best idea!" she exclaimed.

Best friends Sander Loya and Barron James broke into a dance at the news.

"Forget it, Caitlyn." Sander yelled. "We are *so* going to win!"

Brown raised his hands, once again signaling for silence. "There's more. Helping us make these videos will be . . . Nate and Shane from Connect Three!" The two bandmates ran onstage and smiled. "Nate is going to be in charge of one group, and Shane will be in charge of the other."

Nate stepped up to the microphone. "Hi, everyone. Since I can only be here for a few days," he said, "I would like to invite a camper to be my right-hand man on this video. Someone I know just happens to be a whiz with the camera . . . Sander!"

Sander, a huge smile on his face, joined Nate and Shane on the stage. Mitchie grinned, too. That was the great thing about Camp Rock. One day you were an ordinary kid, and the next day you were living your dreams.

Shane looked over at Mitchie and raised

up crossed fingers. She did the same. If she got to be in his group, this session was bound to be off to a good start.

But as Brown took a rumpled sheet of paper out of his pocket and began to read off the groups, Mitchie realized that sometimes dreams just didn't come true.

CHAPTER FOUR

Mitchie looked around at her group. After Brown's announcements, they had gathered in a corner of the mess hall to discuss their strategy. Lorraine and Colby were there. And so were Lola and Ella, along with a few other familiar faces. But Caitlyn, Shane, and Peggy were missing. Pushing aside the sad feeling that threatened to ruin the mood, she instead looked at her leaders—Nate and Sander.

Nate did a short clockwise spin followed by a longer counterclockwise spin. Then he smiled. "That's a dance move I have perfected over the years. Now, I know you all have stuff that you're already great at. But making this video is all about learning how to break out of your comfort zone!" Nate did another, more complicated dance move and promptly fell over. He shrugged. "We can't be afraid to fail at first, because that's the first step to succeeding!"

Everyone nodded. "So," Nate continued, "a video obviously starts with a song, just like Brown said. Once we have that, we can move on to our concept. Dee and Brown want us to present our songs tomorrow. . . ."

"*Tomorrow?*" Sander repeated. "We have to come up with a song by tomorrow?"

Nate nodded. "Anyone got any ideas?"

Silence fell as everyone looked down at the floor.

Mitchie took a deep breath. She couldn't

believe she was about to do this. "I started to write a song today. It's really rough though." She snuck a glance at Colby. If she shared it, would he figure out that their earlier encounter was the inspiration?

"Well, rough is better than what we have—which is nothing," Nate joked. "Let's hear it."

Standing up, Mitchie tried to calm her racing heart. Even though she had managed to sing in front of everyone at Final Jam, performing still made her nervous. Quietly, she sang out the first few lines to what she was calling "Your Little Secrets." When she was done, Nate looked impressed.

"That sounds great," he commented. "We can definitely work with that."

Smiling proudly, Mitchie turned to the group. She was surprised to see Colby writing furiously in a notebook. He stopped and looked up.

"I think I just came up with a bridge," he explained.

"Nice. Why don't you and Mitchie sing it for everyone?" Nate asked.

Mitchie took a deep breath. Walking over, she looked down at Colby's messy handwriting. When she had read through the bridge once, she nodded. He had really captured the feel of her song. I wonder, she thought, if it was easy for him because of the topic?

Mitchie and Colby began to sing. As they went on, their voices got stronger and blended, and Mitchie found herself laying a nice, higher harmony over Colby's honeyed tenor. Lola began to accompany them on the keyboard, and someone else took up a tambourine and followed Lola's lead. Even though it was the group's first time running through the song, they managed to end with a nice flourish.

"Wow!" Mitchie exclaimed when it was over.

"Wow is right," Sander said. "That was great. But you guys should keep practicing.

We want to be as strong as possible by tomorrow night."

As everyone nodded in agreement, Mitchie hesitated. She was supposed to meet up with Caitlyn. And she still hadn't heard Shane's new song. But this was her group. She couldn't bail. "Okay," she agreed. "Let's do it!"

Meanwhile, Shane's team had gathered in a clearing by the lake. The sun was shining, and the water sparkled. It would have been fun to go swimming, but they had work to do.

Peggy and Caitlyn sat on the ground while Barron and Andy leaned against a tree. Tess had grabbed a portable chair and set it up right near Shane so she wouldn't miss a word.

Shane quickly recapped the timeline and what they needed to do. When he was finished, Tess raised her hand.

"I have an idea," she said. "Since Shane has worked with so many great choreographers,

I think we should focus our video on dance. And have Shane in it." Tess shot the group a look, daring them to disagree. Luckily, everyone seemed to like the idea.

Everyone, that is, except Shane. "I don't know," he said hesitantly. "I'm supposed to be teaching, not doing."

"No one said you couldn't be in the video," Tess said. "And I have an amazing routine that we could use."

Time was of the essence. They were supposed to find a song first, but a strong routine might be able to inspire them. It looked like Tess's choice was the only one they had.

Taking the group's silence as an invitation to start, Tess walked to a flat area, Shane following. As everyone watched, Tess showed Shane a routine that was part Latin, part ballroom, with a little dash of hip-hop. He learned it quickly, and soon the two were dipping and swirling and twirling all over the grass. It looked like they'd been dancing together for years.

Caitlyn was impressed. She had expected something showy from Tess. This, though, was different. It was fun but also complex. "Do it again," she said. "I think I have some melodies that you guys can groove to. Andy, why don't you see what kind of rhythm you can add to this? And Peggy, why don't you work on lyrics? We might just have a shot."

Shane was about to agree when he glimpsed movement out of the corner of his eye. Turning, he saw Mitchie running down the steps of the mess hall, laughing. Right next to her was one of the new campers— Colby. Watching them race down the path and into the woods, Shane felt an odd pang. He and Mitchie were supposed to hang out later. So, where was she running off to?

CHAPTER FIVE

Caitlyn knew Camp Rock inside and out. She felt it was part of her duty as a veteran camper to make sure she stayed on top of the latest news and info that passed through the trees, cabins, and fields of the camp. Which was why she was making her way now to B-Note—the camp's canteen—for a much needed gossip fix. And maybe some candy, Caitlyn thought, as her stomach growled.

The canteen was located in the basement of the mess hall and housed treats for anyone who was between care packages. Caitlyn found Lola and Ella lounging on one of the many worn couches strewn about the room. "Hey there," Caitlyn said, making a beeline for the gummi worms. Hmmm . . . she thought. Gummi worms or gummi bears? Or sour gummies? Shaking her head, she grabbed some worms and made her way back to her friends.

"So, how is the video coming?" she asked Lola and Ella.

Ella looked confused. "Video? I thought we were working on a song. If there is going to be a camera, I totally need to get some new lip gloss. Like, now!"

Lola rolled her eyes good-naturedly. Ella was a sweetheart, but she wasn't always the brightest star in the sky. Still, the girl could really sing and was a loyal friend. "We *are* doing a video, silly!" Lola explained. Then, turning to Caitlyn, she added, "We're just in the song part of the process right now."

Caitlyn nodded and bit a piece of candy in half. She had hoped to find Mitchie at the canteen. It would have been good to swap stories and just relax for a little, but her friend was nowhere to be found.

As if reading her thoughts, Lola once again piped up. "Mitchie and Colby, though, are going to make it pretty easy. The two of them are like peas in a pod! Mitchie wrote these great lyrics, and Colby sort of just knew exactly where to take them. It was pretty awesome to watch."

"Yeah, awesome," Ella repeated, nodding her head.

For a moment, Caitlyn didn't say anything. For some reason, the news that Mitchie and Colby were getting along didn't sit well. It wasn't that she didn't want Mitchie to make friends. That was part of camp. But it sounded like she and Colby were making cool music together—and that was something *Caitlyn* was hoping to do with Mitchie this session. Sighing, she shook off the thought. Mitchie was cool. She wouldn't forget that they had talked about finding a new sound. She was just caught up in the competition.

Forcing a smile, she looked over at Lola and Ella. There were more important things to discuss. "So . . . you guys would have loved to see what Tess came up with at our meeting. . . ."

Across camp, inside the Vibe Cabin, Tess was busy doing what she did best—primping. She sat in front of her mirror, brushing her hair. When she was convinced it couldn't get any silkier, she moved on to the next beauty step—moisturizing. After all, just because she was in the middle of the woods didn't mean she shouldn't keep up her appearance. At a place like Camp Rock, you never knew who would drop in, or when. She took out a small bottle and pumped some lotion into her hands. Then she began to delicately apply it to her face.

Sitting on the bunk behind her, Lorraine was sketching in a notepad. While Lorraine liked to sing, she *loved* to design. She made a lot of her own clothes, but her dream was to be a costume designer to the pop stars. A session at Camp Rock was the first step. Here she could meet future stars, and current ones, and hopefully, one day, her wishes would come true.

Lorraine spent every spare minute designing new creations and had even brought two extra trunks of clothes with her for inspiration—just in case one of the campers needed an awesome new costume at the last minute. At the moment, she was caught up in a particularly exciting piece—a long, sequined, off-the-shoulder gown in a deep navy hue. That was why she didn't hear Tess calling her name until the other girl finally shouted, "Lorraine! Hello!"

Startled, Lorraine's pencil slid across the paper, smearing the image. Sighing, she looked up and saw Tess staring at her, a questioning look in her eyes. Tess was by far the coolest person Lorraine had ever met, but she was also the most intimidating. "Sorry, Tess," Lorraine apologized. "What did you say?"

Tess's blue eyes stayed locked on Lorraine. "I was saying," she huffed, "that I think Shane is beginning to come around. Being in his group for this competition is fate! Soon we'll be hanging out all the time. Don't you think?"

Lorraine cocked her head. She hadn't been at Camp Rock that long, but she already knew that Shane and Mitchie were pretty good friends—which seemed to bother Tess. Not because Tess wanted to be friends with Shane specifically, but more because that meant the spotlight wasn't aimed directly at her. Lorraine secretly thought that was a little silly—after all, Tess's mom was T.J. Tyler! She'd had the spotlight on her since birth. But Lorraine didn't dare say that out loud. "That's great! I heard you two totally clicked," she said instead. "Our group is going to have a tough time beating you guys. We don't even have a concept yet."

Tess turned back to look in the mirror. That was music to her ears. "Well, we do, and I'm sure thinking up a song will be a snap. Between Shane and I, we know all the musical inspirations in the biz. We were born for this stuff. Our song is going to be fantastic." She gave Lorraine a satisfied smile.

"I'm sure," Lorraine said, nodding in agreement. "I *so* wish I was in your group. I could totally outfit you. I have this one dress . . ."

Tess didn't let her finish. "Just because we're not in the same group doesn't mean we can't help each other out. Now, what does the dress look like?" she asked, her eyes gleaming.

Lorraine's eyes brightened. Tess wanted to see her dress?! She couldn't believe it. Tess had *the* greatest taste, and if she wore it in the video, everyone would see Lorraine's design! It was great publicity—not to mention it meant Tess had to really consider her a friend.

Meanwhile, Tess was busy plotting her next move. She had already gotten Shane to dance with her. Now she just needed to win the video competition—and then next stop: ultimate fame and glory! Maybe she and Shane could even get a spot on that hot new dance show her mom's assistant was telling her about. And maybe, Tess thought, if I do well on the show. . .

Tess snapped herself out of the daydream. Ever since her mom had come to Final Jam and barely paid attention, Tess had wanted a chance to have a serious heart-to-heart with her and tell her how hurt she had been. But T.J. was always too busy, which meant the only correspondence Tess received was an occasional e-mail or postcard sent through her mom's assistant.

Pushing back her shoulders, Tess took a deep breath. Final Jam had been a bust, but this competition was her next chance. She would figure out a way to talk to her mom after her group had won.

CHAPTER SIX

Mitchie trotted along one of the many paths that crisscrossed Camp Rock, humming to herself. She had been happy when camp started, but now that it was in full swing, she was on cloud nine. It felt like every minute was an adventure. And now that she had an hour break from camp activities, she was off to find Shane.

Hearing footsteps behind her, she turned.

Colby was jogging up the path, a big smile on his face.

"Having fun so far?" she asked when he reached her. "It's pretty magical, right?"

Colby's smile disappeared. "Magic isn't real," he said quietly.

Mitchie looked over at him curiously, but she didn't say anything. They walked in silence for a few minutes. Suddenly, Colby stopped. "Hey, do you want to sit down?"

They were standing next to the bench beside the hollowed-out tree. Mitchie paused. Should she tell him this was where she and Shane hung out? Would it sound like she was bragging? Would Colby even care? Shaking off her doubts, Mitchie nodded and they sat down.

Colby gazed down at his shoes and silently kicked a rock. Just when the silence had stretched into the realm of awkward, he spoke. "So, uh, you saw me earlier, right? Talking to my dad?" he asked nervously.

Mitchie nodded, remembering the man in the truck. "I guess you figured out that he isn't exactly psyched to have me going here."

Mitchie felt a rush of sympathy. Her parents were so supportive of her music. It was hard to imagine what her life would be like if they weren't.

Colby continued, "It's not that my dad doesn't like music. I mean, he does. We listen to the radio all the time while we're working." Noticing Mitchie's confused look, he explained, "My dad builds sailboats, and my younger brother and I help out in the summer. My brother totally loves it, but I'd rather be playing my guitar."

"So then it's good you're here," Mitchie said encouragingly. "He let you come . . . that's got to mean something, right?"

Colby shook his head. Should he really be telling Mitchie all of this? He barely knew her. But there was something warm in her smile, and if he didn't tell someone, he was sure he'd explode. He took a deep breath. "It's not that simple. He could pick me up at any moment. The only reason he let me come in the first place is because we weren't that busy. But if he gets a lot of work, he'll be packing my bags—no matter if he lost money on tuition. Even if I was having a great time, I don't think it would really matter."

"Well, he's not here yet. So let's not worry about it until we see his truck," Mitchie pointed out. Colby's frown began to fade as she added, "Plus, we have a song to practice and a winning video to make. This is no time to get bummed out."

"Thanks, Mitchie," Colby said warmly. "Let's just keep this between us, if you don't mind. I know we haven't known each other long, but you seem like someone who knows how to keep a secret. And I wouldn't want people to treat me funny. . . ." His voice trailed off.

"Of course," Mitchie promised. Then she

frowned. Shane! She had gotten completely sidetracked. She stood up and dusted off her shorts.

"Everything all right?" Colby asked.

"Sure," Mitchie said absently. "It's just I was supposed to meet Shane, and now I'm superlate."

"Shane Gray?" Colby asked. "He seems so cool, to come back here and help out. I'd love to have a career like that."

Mitchie nodded. Shane was lucky—but he'd also worked hard and overcome a lot this summer.

Waving good-bye to Colby, she headed down the path and nearly collided with Tess.

"Hey! Watch where you are going!" Tess snapped. Her eyes darted past Mitchie and landed on Colby. "Oh. I hope I didn't interrupt anything," she said, raising an eyebrow.

"No, not at all," Mitchie said. "Colby and I were just talking."

"Well," Tess said. "It's good that you're getting to know each other. This session is all about new friendships. Speaking of which, I need to meet my group. It is so great getting to know all of them. Especially Shane!" She shot Mitchie a smug look.

But Mitchie simply smiled. She wasn't going to take the bait. She had seen the softer side of Tess. It might take the rest of the summer, but she was determined to be friends—or at least friendly—with Tess. "Have fun," Mitchie called, hurrying off. Hopefully she'd have time to catch Shane before his group meeting.

In his room in Brown's cabin, Shane was lying on the bed and looking up at the ceiling. Just then, Nate walked in and looked at his friend with concern.

"What's wrong with you?" he asked, flicking a guitar pick at Shane.

Shane sat up and gazed out the window.

He hoped he would see Mitchie coming down the path to see him, but no one was there. Sighing, he looked back at Nate. "You know how earlier you asked why I wanted you to come up here?" Nate nodded. He'd been waiting all day for an answer to that question. "Well, I was going to tell Mitchie something but I totally froze up."

"*That's* the big mystery!" Nate teased. "Not that I'm not having a good time surrounded by insects and bears. But it seems like you're freaking out over nothing. What were you going to tell her? That you like hanging out with her?"

Shane was shocked. Nate had just read him as easily as he would have read a page of sheet music. "Yeah. Well, sort of. I just wanted her to know that it's not just Camp Rock that has made me clean up my act. It's Mitchie, too."

Nate nodded approvingly. "That's great, Shane. So just tell her. She'll be flattered.

Plus, the longer you keep it in, the weirder you're going to feel about saying anything."

Outside the window, a twig snapped and Sander walked into view. "Hey," Shane said. "Have you seen Mitchie?"

"I saw her back on the path with Colby," Sander answered. "They're probably working on our song."

Shane nodded and said good-bye as Nate and Sander headed out to prep their group for that night's song presentation. But despite the smile, Shane was worried. He'd developed his sound here. Now Mitchie and Colby were developing theirs. It was only fair. But if it was fair, why did it make him feel so uneasy?

CHAPTER SEVEN

As the sun began to set, excitement filled the air. Each team was busy getting ready to present the song they planned to use in the video. Only a few campers from each group would actually sing and perform. The rest were in charge of the other aspects of the video, such as wardrobe or lights. Those campers gathered in front of the lakeside stage, eager for the show to begin.

On one side of the stage, Mitchie stood, a microphone clutched in her hand. Colby was standing next to her. He was as white as a ghost.

"Don't be nervous," Mitchie said. "It gets easier. The first time I got on a stage here, they had to recue my music because the words just wouldn't come out."

"Oh, I'm not nervous about performing, really," Colby replied. "The only thing that makes me nervous is the idea of leaving. But you know . . . my dad *does* respect success. Maybe if we can win this video competition, he'll let me stay."

Mitchie smiled. There was a note of confidence in Colby's voice she hadn't heard before. "There's the spirit!" she said. "Camp Rock video: first stop! Next up? MTV!"

Colby was laughing at the thought when Brown finally walked out onto the stage. Everyone got quiet as he picked up the microphone. "I think it's time we get the show started.

First up, we have Mitchie Torres and one of our camp newbies—Colby Miller. They'll be singing an original song composed by . . ."

"By our whole team—and a clarinet Mitchie heard in the woods!" Sander yelled from his seat. "In a very random manner!"

Brown laughed. "There you have it. Take it away!"

The pair took their spots in the middle of the stage as the lights came up. Mitchie smiled as everyone clapped. Then she opened her mouth, and the words just poured out. She felt good onstage, sharing her feelings and her dreams, and when her voice harmonized with Colby's, she felt as if she were floating. Their eyes met as they sang the final note, and they grinned. "We did it," Colby whispered as the audience burst into applause.

On the other side of the stage, Tess and Shane were waiting to go on. Shane watched

Mitchie as she sang, admiring her newfound stage presence.

Noting his gaze, Tess stifled a frown. She needed Shane's attention on winning—*and* her. A lot was riding on this competition for Tess. And if that meant getting Shane's head away from Mitchie, she'd do what it took.

"They sound good together, don't they?" Tess asked.

Shane's eyes shifted and fell on Colby. "I guess. Colby seems a little nervous," he said. Realizing he was being critical for no reason, he added, "Mitchie will calm him down. She is really good at that." Shane frowned and looked at Mitchie and Colby. They had just finished, and the audience was clapping. He watched as Colby leaned over and whispered something in Mitchie's ear. She threw back her head and laughed.

"Shane, you look upset," Tess observed. Before she could figure out a way to use that to her advantage, Brown's voice boomed out over the loudspeakers. It was time for them to go on.

The song the group had created to go with the routine was called "Swing Time." Shane and Tess sounded polished and even though they weren't dancing, it was clear the song was made for movement.

"Great job, great job!" Brown cheered when the music and applause faded. "Now let's get everyone in their respective groups. We're going to have a little critiquing session to give you direction for your videos. Anyone want to start?"

For a moment, nobody said anything as they thought back on the two songs. Finally, Shane stood up. "I just want to say that I thought Colby and Mitchie sounded great together."

Mitchie and Colby began to smile.

"But . . ." Shane went on, "while I think the song is good, I'm not sure that Colby has the star quality needed for a music video."

Mitchie watched as Colby turned bright red. She knew she was blushing as well. Why would Shane say something like that? This was supposed to be constructive criticism. And Shane's comment was kind of . . . mean.

A few more campers added their thoughts, and then Brown brought the night to an end. But not before telling them to keep practicing—they would start on the videos the next day.

On the way back to her cabin, Mitchie walked by Shane. He was talking to Brown in low, serious tones. He caught her eye. Mitchie waited for him to give a sign that he saw her and wanted to talk. But he didn't. It was like she was invisible.

Shane was on the front porch of Brown's cabin strumming his guitar later that evening when Nate walked up the path. Taking a seat, he looked at his bandmate curiously. "Why did you tell Colby he didn't have what it took to be in a video?" he asked. "There was no reason to attack him."

Shane stopped strumming his guitar and sighed. "I was just trying to help."

"You have a really funny way of showing it," Nate replied. "He is good, Shane. But he's not better than you. So why cut him down?"

Shane knew Nate was waiting for an answer, but he didn't know what to say. Through the trees he could see a corner of the lake. He thought about the time he and Mitchie had gone out on the water last session, how peaceful it had been. They had paddled the canoe—in circles—and just laughed. It seemed like a long time ago. "I may have been a *little* hard on Colby," he finally confessed. "But I didn't . . . I didn't do it on purpose. It just sort of happened. I guess I was just jealous of him—because of how good he and Mitchie sounded. And you know the industry. Harsh is part of it."

Nate nodded. But he knew Shane wasn't

overreacting because of the industry. Shane had overcome a lot already this summer— with Mitchie's help. And while he may be confident on the stage, out in the woods, it seemed Shane Gray was more unsure of himself.

"Look, do me a favor," Nate finally said. "Just talk to Colby, would you? Apologize, maybe. I don't want his confidence to be shot."

Shane nodded. "I will."

Nate finally smiled. "That's the great thing about you," he said. "You admit it when you do something wrong. Look, tomorrow I am out of here. No more life coach. No more free advice. So remember—apologize to Colby and talk to Mitchie. You'll feel better for it. I am counting on you to do the right thing. I know you will."

Shane tried to smile. He hoped Nate was right.

CHAPTER EIGHT

The next morning, Mitchie was up bright and early for kitchen duty. Walking around the cabin, she noticed Caitlyn's bed was already made. That's odd, Mitchie thought. Caitlyn hates waking up early. I wonder what she's up to? Shrugging, Mitchie threw on a yellow shirt and khaki skirt. Then, she ran to the kitchen.

When she arrived, much to her surprise,

Caitlyn was already there, her laptop open on the counter.

"Hey," Caitlyn said. "I figured since you seem awfully busy, that early morning might be the only time to hang out and work on our music." She didn't add that it was beginning to really bother her, or that it seemed like Mitchie was always making time for Colby.

Mitchie frowned. Caitlyn's voice had a hard edge. Mitchie couldn't really blame her. She *had* been kind of wrapped up in her group. They'd been working practically nonstop. The only time she had seen Caitlyn was in their cabin right before lights-out. "Good plan," Mitchie said cheerfully, hoping to lighten the mood. "Strike up the band!"

But it was not to be. A knock at the door interrupted them. Looking over, Mitchie saw Colby.

"Hey," he said, smiling at both girls. Mitchie broke into a broad grin, but Caitlyn just nodded and looked down at her computer.

Figures, Caitlyn thought. Wherever Mitchie goes, Colby follows. He's like her shadow.

Unaware of Caitlyn's thoughts, Mitchie held out a glass of orange juice. "Here," she said. "OJ is always a good way to start a Camp Rock morning."

"Will this cure a bruised ego?" Colby asked, taking it.

Mitchie knew exactly what he was talking about. "Don't be bummed about last night," she said. "It's just one person's opinion."

"Yeah, but that one person happens to be one of the coolest pop stars in the world," he pointed out.

Mitchie felt a rush of sympathy for Colby, followed by an unfamiliar flash of anger toward Shane. He'd been so harsh. She wanted to talk to him and see if he could explain. But he'd been ignoring her. "Listen," Mitchie said gently. "You can't take what every star or record executive says personally, or you'll never make it in the music business. You have to make me a deal, okay?" Colby nodded and Mitchie went on. "From now on, we only focus on the music. Forget about Shane and just enjoy your·time here. Now, take a sip of your juice to seal the deal."

Colby was laughing when Lola and Lorraine suddenly came running into the kitchen. They fell against the door, panting.

"Geez," Mitchie joked. "This isn't a sports camp all of a sudden, is it?"

"No, better! We just found out that Gillian DeRose is coming here today! To Camp Rock!" Lola cried. "She's going to consult and advise on the videos!"

Everyone—even Caitlyn—gasped. Gillian was one of the best video directors in the business. The competition had just gotten a lot more serious.

Gillian DeRose was a compact woman with long, dark hair. She wore a black tracksuit and matching baseball cap. She looked all business as she paced up and down the mess hall in front of Mitchie and the rest of her group.

"What's your song about?" Gillian asked after introducing herself.

Nobody spoke.

Realizing no one wanted to go first, Mitchie held up her hand. "You don't need to raise your hand," Gillian barked. "Do you think artists—real artists—are afraid to speak up?"

Mitchie's cheeks turned red. Taking a deep breath she explained, "The song is called 'Your Little Secrets.' It's about the stuff that we keep bottled up inside. The stuff we are afraid to share or think no one will under-stand. It's about figuring out that sometimes it helps to talk." An image of Shane flashed through her mind. He had opened up to her, and she hadn't even made the time to see him since the new session had started.

Sighing, Mitchie waited to hear Gillian's response.

Gillian nodded. "That's a solid start. Now, a great video enhances the song it is made for. Does anyone have any ideas for concepts that would do that?"

There was a pause. Then people started to shout out ideas excitedly.

"A bunch of people whispering to each other!" Lola suggested.

"They could totally be playing that game, telephone, where they talk into the cans," Ella added.

"I know," Lorraine said. "A bunch of people are just walking past each other, not saying what's on their minds, but, like, over their heads you can tell what they're thinking."

"That's a great idea," Gillian praised.

Lorraine beamed.

"Unfortunately, it's already been done," Gillian added, frowning. "To make it in this business, you need a lot more than a good voice. You need fresh ideas. Get some. I am supposed to consult, not do your work for you." Her speech over, Gillian turned on one heel and left the mess hall. Two assistants, dressed exactly like Gillian, each walking an identical French bulldog, quickly followed her out the door.

"Whoa!" Colby exclaimed after she was gone. "And I thought my dad was tough."

"Whoa is right," said Mitchie. "Gillian is way intense."

"But maybe that's a good thing," Colby said. "I'm convinced that if we can win this thing, I might be able to get my dad to let me stay. And with her help . . ."

"Hey," Mitchie said, interrupting him. "What did we talk about? Forget the future. We have to focus on the fun here and now."

Colby laughed. "You're right. How could I doubt you?"

Mitchie gave her friend a playful nudge on

the arm. She tried to look upbeat. But on the inside, she knew this challenge was going to get harder before it got any easier. And if things didn't work out, Colby could go home.

Mitchie was back on kitchen duty, preparing lunch. She was grating cheese for the tacos that were on the menu that day when Caitlyn walked in. Caitlyn absently picked up a grater and began running a wedge of cheese over its sharp edges. The room filled with an uncomfortable silence.

"Gee, grating cheese is a workout, huh?" Mitchie asked, struggling for something to say.

Caitlyn shrugged but didn't respond.

Mitchie stifled a sigh. It seemed that lately she couldn't make anyone happy. Upset, she said the first thing that came to mind. "I'm kind of worried about Colby."

Caitlyn's shoulders stiffened. "Worried? You barely know him."

"That's not true!" Mitchie cried defensively. She had spent a lot of time with Colby over the past few days. *And* he had confided in her about his family. But maybe Caitlyn was right. She didn't know him as well as she knew Caitlyn or Shane. Still . . . "I know that he's under a lot of pressure," she finished lamely.

"Maybe you should be worried about your old friends," Caitlyn snapped. "We were supposed to work together this session, remember? And then you just drop me. Same old Mitchie—always falling for the new thing."

Caitlyn's words hurt—mostly because she was right. I *have* been kind of preoccupied, Mitchie thought.

Taking a deep breath, Mitchie looked Caitlyn in the eye. "I was just trying to help Colby, the way you helped me when I first came to camp," she said sincerely. "But I promise, from now on I'm going to try and be here for you, too."

"Promise?" Caitlyn said.

"Promise," Mitchie said, crossing a finger over her heart.

The two friends smiled.

"We've been having some problems getting a concept together for the contest, but once we do I'm going to be free and clear," Mitchie added.

Caitlyn nodded. Then a sly smile spread across her face. "I think you have much bigger problems. We're going to have to figure out what to do about this," she said.

Mitchie looked down and started laughing. They'd been so caught up in their conversation, they had created a mountain of grated cheese. It looked like taco night was going to be heavy on the dairy.

CHAPTER NINE

After lunch, the groups once again split up to discuss their videos. Gathered in a corner of the mess hall, Sander looked at his team. "All right, everyone. Nate is gone," he said, causing them all to groan. "But that doesn't mean we give up. I've been thinking, and I have a concept that Gillian might be okay with." When he was sure he had everyone's attention, he went on. "We film down on the beach, but we make it look like a deserted island. There are a bunch of people—played by us—stranded. All of them are scared and want to get rescued but instead of working together and sharing their fears, they work alone. At the end of the video, they realize that the only way for them to be saved is to share their secrets and ideas and work together."

As Sander spoke, Mitchie's heart began to race. This concept sounded perfect! She looked around her group. Everyone was nodding. It was official, the idea was a hit.

Grabbing his camera, Sander led the group down to the beach to begin filming. He wanted to get some establishing shots. Once the scene was set, Mitchie and Colby would have to incorporate the singing.

Lola and Ella began building two bonfires on separate ends of the beach. Colby lay on his back, gazing up at the sky. Lorraine spelled out HELP in the sand.

Mitchie watched, a pit starting to grow in

her stomach. Everyone else had ideas, and Mitchie had none. She was having video block! Just when she thought it was hopeless, something popped into her head. Using a blanket, she ran up and down the beach, waving for help.

When Sander had enough shots, he cued the music. With the camera rolling, Colby and Mitchie began to sing. More accurately, *Colby* began to sing. "Just pretend I'm not here," Sander said, starting over. But no matter how hard she tried, Mitchie couldn't perform. She felt so awkward.

Finally, after what felt like hours, Mitchie was able to get through the song once without sounding too awful. Satisfied that they had enough to work with, Sander stopped recording and they headed back to the mess hall to show Gillian their video. She was waiting for them, her assistants and dogs beside her.

"She changed," Lorraine whispered to Mitchie, noting a tracksuit identical to the previous one except for its color. This one was pink. "Do you think that will make her less scary?"

"I hope so," Mitchie said.

"Hello," Gillian said when the group was settled. Sander gave her a little wave on everyone's behalf. Gillian pursed her lips impatiently and checked the big gold watch on her wrist. "Okay, lights down, film up," she demanded. "We're on a very tight deadline!"

Sander had attached the video camera to a TV set up in the corner. He pressed PLAY.

Mitchie watched, trying to pretend it wasn't her and her friends on the screen. But that wasn't easy. With so little time, they hadn't been able to work on the sound. And Mitchie was convinced no one in the history of video-making had ever looked as strange on camera as she did.

As Gillian watched the video, she paced. When the screen faded to black, she stopped short. "Not bad," she commented.

"I heard that 'not bad' from her is like 'You're a shoe-in for the VMA's' from anyone else," Lola whispered to Mitchie.

But then Gillian snapped, "The girl with the blanket—identify yourself!"

"That's, ah, uh, me," Mitchie stammered, trying to keep her voice steady.

"You have a good voice," Gillian said. Mitchie started to smile. "But since you're singing lead, you're the one who is central in the video. And that performance will just not do."

Mitchie's smile disappeared, and her cheeks grew hot as everyone turned to look at her. Fighting back tears, she said, "Uh, I can try harder."

Gillian opened up her designer handbag and began rummaging around in it. "I'm not sure trying harder will work," she said icily. "If you want to win, you'd better get good—fast." With those words echoing in the room, Gillian turned and left.

There was nothing more to do. The rest of the group began to leave, too. But before Mitchie could run out, Sander pulled her aside. "Hey, don't take it too hard," he said gently. "A lot of people aren't naturally good on camera. But they can be. You have to break through and find your inner video star."

"But how?" Mitchie asked, looking into Sander's kind eyes. He put a sympathetic hand on her arm.

He shrugged. "I don't know. You're going to have to figure that out yourself."

Shane needed to clear his head. Heading for the docks, he thought about the past few days. When he had found out Mitchie was "the voice" at Final Jam, he had been convinced it was the beginning of something great. But things weren't great. They were all messed up.

He walked with his head down onto the smooth wood of the dock. Looking up, he saw Mitchie leaning against a canoe.

"Hey," he said. "I didn't think anyone would be down here."

Mitchie saw the hesitation in Shane's eyes. "Do you want me to go?" she asked.

"Oh, no," he answered quickly. That was the last thing he wanted. "So, uh, are you having fun working with Gillian?" he asked, trying to make conversation.

Mitchie just shrugged.

"She is pretty amazing. We worked with her on one of our first videos," Shane went on. Mitchie still didn't say anything. "She really sees things other people miss."

She obviously sees how bad an actress I am, Mitchie thought. She wanted to share her fears with Shane, but he had been acting so strange lately. So, instead, she asked how his group's video was going.

"It's going fine," he said. "Tess and I are working really well together. I heard you and Colby really hit it off, too." As soon as the words were out of his mouth, he wished he could take them back.

But Mitchie didn't seem upset at all. In fact, she didn't even seem to be paying attention. She just nodded and smiled. "I'm glad it's going well," she said. Getting up, she brushed off her jeans. "Well, I should get back to my group," she said, careful not to let her voice betray the fact that she *had* been paying attention and was upset. "See you later, Shane." And before he could say a word, she walked away.

Listening to the sound of the water lap against the wooden dock, Shane just stood there, utterly confused. What had just happened?

Sander was taking his job as director very seriously. He walked around the beach, camera in hand, barking orders. "Smiles with the bonfires. Smiles!" he called out to Lola and Ella. "Let's really carve that message into the sand, Lorraine. We want the planes to be able to read it!" He grinned at Mitchie, who was standing next to him, blanket clutched in her hand. "You think I can get a chair with my name on it, and a megaphone?" he asked playfully.

Mitchie grinned, despite how nervous she was feeling. "If we win, you can have both," she said. "But I'm afraid until we make it to the big time, you're just going to have to yell really loud."

"*If* we win!?" he cried. "We *are* going to win!"

Mitchie didn't bother to point out that they might not—because of her. Instead, she took a deep breath and began running up and down the beach, waving the blanket as she mouthed the words to their song.

But no matter how hard she tried, she couldn't get Gillian's words out of her mind. The more she tried to look good on camera, the more insecure she felt. She thought she was going to burst into tears, but she knew that *really* wouldn't look good. When Sander finally called for a ten-minute break, Mitchie sat down and sank into the warm sand gratefully.

Colby plopped down next to her. "You look bummed," he said. "If I didn't know you better, I'd think you really were stuck on a desert island."

"I might as well be. I'm all alone . . . in being horrible!" Mitchie blurted out.

"What does Sander say?" Colby asked.

"He says I can get better. I just need to," she made quote marks in the air, " 'break through.' "

Colby nodded. "My dad always tells me that even if I don't like making boats, I should act like I do. If I do it long enough, he says, eventually I'll believe it. But for some people, people like us, I think, it's really hard to just pretend."

Mitchie nodded. Colby was right. Pretending she wasn't afraid was going to be hard. But with so much on the line, she was going to have to try.

Inside the Beat cabin, Caitlyn sat waiting for Mitchie. They were supposed to meet during one of the group breaks. But it had been over an hour, and Mitchie still hadn't shown. Shutting her laptop, Caitlyn headed to the beach, hoping she might run into her friend there.

As she approached the lake, she heard people laughing. Walking along the shore were Mitchie and Colby.

Caitlyn almost yelled hello. But then she stopped herself. Even though she was only a few feet away, she felt miles from Mitchie. So much for promises, Caitlyn thought. I guess all that talk in the kitchen meant nothing.

For the first time since the new session had started, Caitlyn wished she'd gone home. At least there she knew who her friends were.

CHAPTER TEN

Tess stood inside one of the vacant cabins that Brown had set aside for excess luggage and stared at a glorious site—two whole trunks full of fantastic, glittery, sparkly, beautiful costumes. And all of them were Lorraine's. Which meant all of them could be hers . . . at least for the video shoot.

She turned and looked thoughtfully at Lorraine. In the hazy light of the cabin, her red hair looked darker than usual and her freckles were barely visible. She was usually shy and a bit quiet, but now, surrounded by her creations, Lorraine was like a whole new person.

"And this one," Lorraine said, picking up a silk bundle, "was one I thought would work for a salsa number." She held it up. The dress was a paisley combination of green, white, and black on the skirt. And the top was a simple black halter that accented the fun print. It looked perfect for twirling and whirling around a stage.

"It's beautiful," Tess gushed. "I didn't know you were so talented."

Lorraine's cheeks turned as red as her hair. "Th-thanks," she stuttered. "It's fun, and when things are busy or I just need to get my head on straight . . . sewing and creating, it just makes me feel good. It's like when you take the stage, right?" she asked.

For a moment, Tess didn't respond. Was that the feeling she was supposed to have when she was on the stage? Usually she was so busy looking to see if her mother had joined the audience, she didn't think about anything but that. Still, if she thought about it, there *was* a feeling of peace that came with performing. Nodding, she smiled. "That's exactly how I feel. And I'm going to feel even better when I'm wearing one of your costumes. So, what else do you have?"

Lorraine gave Tess a wide smile and reached back into the trunk. She had a lot of dresses to sort through and a short amount of time to do it. But she would find Tess the perfect outfit . . . she was sure of it.

After stopping by the kitchen to check in with her mom, Mitchie was heading back to her cabin. Walking by the hollowed-out tree, she she saw a foot poking out from inside. "Hello," she called.

Colby's head popped out. When he saw Mitchie, he smiled.

"Hey!" Mitchie cried. "What are you doing in there?"

"I thought of a way to make you feel better about the camera," he said with a grin. "I figured you might walk by here, so I thought I'd try and catch you." Reaching into a bag next to him, he pulled out two costumes—a clown suit and a werewolf outfit. "Ready to make a fool of yourself?"

Mitchie laughed. "Where did you get those?" Did Colby actually expect her to put one of those on?

Apparently, he did. "The important thing isn't where I got them," Colby replied. "It's what we're going to do with them. You want to be the werewolf or the clown?"

"I'll be the clown," she said, shrugging.

"I guess that makes me the werewolf," he said with a wink and started pulling the costume on over his clothes. He handed her the clown suit. "Here, you put that on. Now let's go talk to people. If this doesn't help you get over being camera shy, then I don't know what will."

Michie gave Colby a hesitant look but followed him. They went all over Camp Rock. They went to the lake and heckled the people swimming. They went to the tennis courts. Colby howled, and Mitchie juggled some old tennis balls.

When they got to the mess hall, they found Shane's team outside, practicing. Shane and Tess were dancing, and Caitlyn was frowning over her computer as she tried to find the perfect backbeat. "I don't want to bother them," Mitchie whispered.

"You're not *you*, you're a clown!" Colby reminded her.

Easier said than done, she thought. Colby wasn't here earlier this summer. He doesn't know what happened, or that I spent a lot of time pretending to be someone I'm not. Still, that was then. This is now.

Taking a deep breath, Mitchie ran up and

started to juggle three rocks—or at least she tried. Everyone stopped what they were doing and stared. Mitchie kept juggling as Colby ran in circles around her, howling. Slowly the group began to smile and then laugh. Soon everyone was cheering on the two.

Everyone that is, except Caitlyn and Shane. Caitlyn clamped her headphones over her ears and wouldn't look at Colby and Mitchie, while Shane stared at them, confused.

"Mitchie, what are you doing?" Shane asked.

She was about to answer when Colby came up to her. "You can't break character," he said through his werewolf mask. "It's part of the exercise! Now come on! We have to take this act back on the road."

Shooting Shane an apologetic look, Mitchie ran off. Finally they made it back to the tree. Mitchie couldn't stop laughing as she took her red nose off. "I've never done anything so ridiculous," she said after she caught her breath.

"You're going to be a lot more relaxed in front of the camera now," he said. "I promise. It can't be any scarier than what we just did. A camera can't laugh at you."

Mitchie smiled. "Thanks, Colby."

"Anytime," he replied. "It's the least I can do. You helped me forget about my father—even if for a little while. Now, let's go get rid of these costumes. They're hot!"

Colby was right. When their group met before dinner to film the video, Mitchie was ready. Before, she had felt like the camera was an actual, live thing just waiting for her to do something wrong. But this time she didn't even notice it. She ran around, waving her blanket, imagining that she really was stranded on an island. When Sander called, "Cut," Mitchie breathed a sigh of relief. Colby had saved the day. She might not be a bona fide video star, but there was no way Gillian could hate that performance—she hoped.

CHAPTER ELEVEN

After dinner that evening, Sander's team filed into the camp's canteen to watch the latest cut of their video. They settled into the couches and chairs set up in front of the screen, grinning from ear to ear as they waited for Gillian. She arrived ten minutes late, her assistants and dogs in town.

Before the footage rolled, she gave them what passed as her version of a pep talk. "As you know, Shane's team has always had a strong concept. But you have a great song. Let's hope this video helps make it even better. We want everyone to look dynamic on camera. No stragglers." She raised an eyebrow at Mitchie.

Mitchie's heart jumped. Reaching over, Colby squeezed her shoulder. "Don't even worry about it," he whispered. "You were awesome." Mitchie smiled gratefully.

As the video began, Mitchie watched intently, trying to imagine that she was seeing it for the first time. The group looked good, but something was off. Everyone looked *too* happy. Keeping secrets bottled up wasn't supposed to be a good thing. "It's like it goes with another song," she whispered to Colby.

"Nah," he said. "We're just too close to it."

But when the lights came back on, Gillian was frowning. "I have some good news and some bad news," she said slowly. She looked at Mitchie. "I don't know how you did it, but you look one-hundred-percent better on camera."

Mitchie nodded appreciatively. Moments ago, that was all she had wanted to hear. But that was before Gillian had mentioned "bad news." She held her breath, waiting.

"But the bad news is that the video concept isn't working," Gillian said flatly.

Sander let out a groan. "Are you sure we can't just tweak it?"

"If by tweak," Gillian retorted, "you mean do it all over again, then yes." She checked the big black watch on her wrist. "We need something new—in the next twenty-four hours. Or else you can forget about winning."

After Gillian left, the group sat in stunned silence. They had worked so hard—for nothing. They were back at square one.

"Let's all take a break," Sander said. "Sometimes getting distance makes for better ideas."

The group stood up and began to leave. "Want to go down to the lake and relax?" Lola asked Mitchie as they filed out of the room.

Mitchie wanted to say yes, but she didn't even have the energy to relax. She needed some TLC. Saying good-bye, she headed toward the mess hall—and her mom.

Connie Torres was pulling a batch of peanut butter cookies out of the oven when Mitchie walked through the door.

Seeing the look on her daughter's face, Connie's eyes filled with alarm. "Oh, no!" she cried. "What did Gillian say?" Mitchie had filled her in on Gillian during breakfast prep. Her mom was well aware of the director, her dogs, *and* her opinions.

Mitchie sat down and bit into a warm cookie. "She said I looked good on camera and that I had obviously conquered my fear."

Connie sat down next to Mitchie. "And why

has this good news made you so miserable?"

Mitchie took another bite. "Now she says we have to come up with a whole new concept for our video. Sometimes I think she'll only be happy if we win the video competition. Which is weird, since she's helping the other group, too."

Her mom sighed. "It would be nice if you won, sweetie, but that shouldn't be your only goal. Plus, you already have won, in a way. You learned how to be comfortable in front of a camera."

Mitchie shrugged. "I guess so," she said. But there was so much more at stake than simply winning a competition. If they lost and Colby's dad wanted him to come home, he'd have his excuse. How could she explain to her mom—who was so supportive—about Colby's father. She couldn't. Plus, she had promised Colby she wouldn't say anything. So instead she said, "I just wish I felt more inspired."

"Maybe you need to start hanging out with a new crowd," another voice answered icily. Turning, Mitchie saw that Caitlyn had come into the kitchen.

Aware of the tension in the air, Connie stood up. "I think I'm going to go see what supplies we need," she said.

After her mom left, Mitchie turned to Caitlyn. "You're right. About the crowd I mean. My group's at a complete dead end," she admitted. "We can't think of anything."

Caitlyn sighed. After Mitchie had blown her off the previous day, Caitlyn had vowed not to seek her out. But she missed her friend. And seeing Mitchie so upset, her anger faded. "Can't think of anything? What about a video about a werewolf and a clown that can't juggle?"

Mitchie laughed.

"Listen," Caitlyn said, growing serious. "I know the competition is making things tense. But *everyone* is tense. You aren't in this alone. You have to remember that you can ask for help—especially from your friends."

"But . . . but why would you want to help me?" Mitchie asked. "It's a competition."

"Well," Caitlyn replied, "if you don't have a video, it's not going to be much of one. Come with me."

Mitchie followed Caitlyn down the hall and into one of the supply closets. Caitlyn sat down on a crate and pulled another out for Mitchie. "This is where I go to shut out the world," Caitlyn told her. "And you need to do the same."

Mitchie sat down. Despite how stressed out she was, Mitchie felt herself starting to relax. "Close your eyes," Caitlyn commanded. "I want you to think about what inspired you to write this song in the first place. What it really means."

Mitchie closed her eyes. She thought about Colby standing by his dad's truck. She thought about how sad and alone he had looked—as if he had no one to share his feelings with.

"Getting any ideas?" Caitlyn said.

Mitchie nodded slowly. "Maybe. The song is all about having to keep the best parts of yourself secret," Mitchie said. Another moment flashed through her mind—Colby in the kitchen, seeking her out. "It's not worth it," she heard Colby say. "I'm just going to have to go home."

Mitchie's eyes sprang open. "I might have an idea!" she exclaimed, standing up.

Caitlyn smiled. "You going to share?"

"I can't," Mitchie answered. "Not yet. I need to find Colby first."

Caitlyn's smile disappeared instantly and was replaced by a deep frown. "I should have known," she said, her voice flat. "It's always about Colby."

"That's not true!" Mitchie cried. But before she could explain, Caitlyn turned and walked out into the hall. Feeling guilty all over again, Mitchie followed her.

But when she got outside, she saw Colby racing down one of the paths that led to the mess hall. His face was pale. "My dad just called!" he cried when he reached Mitchie. "He's coming to get me. He's on his way right now!"

"What?" Mitchie cried. "But you just got here! We haven't even finished the video competition!"

As she stood there, processing the bad news, Shane walked by, looking for his group. Noticing their expressions, he came over. "What's going on?"

Mitchie wanted to tell him what was happening, but it was too late now. She had told Colby his secret was safe. She and Colby would have to deal with it on their own. "It's nothing," Mitchie replied, trying to sound convincing. "Just something's come up and I need to help Colby."

A look of hurt flashed across Shane's face.

Caitlyn had overheard the entire conversation. She came over and put a hand on Shane's shoulder. "Forget it," she said. "Mitchie doesn't have time for us anymore."

"It's not like that!" Mitchie cried. "Caitlyn, I totally appreciate your helping me just now. . . ."

Caitlyn just crossed her arms in front of her chest and ignored Mitchie.

"Shane," Mitchie said, turning to him, "you have to understand. . . ."

"Don't bother," Shane said. "You don't care. I get it."

"Of course I care!" But even as she said it, Mitchie was turning to follow Colby, who had started down the path. "Look. I just have to deal with this. I promise, I will come find you later."

"Who are you talking to?" Shane asked.

"Both of you," Mitchie called back over her shoulder.

"It doesn't matter," Caitlyn said. "She doesn't mean it either way."

CHAPTER TWELVE

After Mitchie left, Caitlyn headed back inside. She needed a cookie. Walking slowly into the kitchen, she saw that Mitchie's mom had returned.

Noticing Caitlyn's glum expression, Connie's mothering instincts went into high gear. Something was going on, and she wanted to get to the bottom of it. This was camp! It was supposed to be fun and easy. "You okay, sweetie?" she asked gently.

Caitlyn felt her face redden. She felt so embarrassed. But, it would be good to talk to someone. She took a deep breath. "I don't know," she began. "I just feel like Mitchie has totally forgotten about me. About everyone but Colby."

Connie sighed. So *that* was what was going on. "I know she has been distracted," she said. "But she hasn't forgotten you. Mitchie's a loyal friend. Back in our hometown, she's had the same best friend for years."

Caitlyn shrugged, unconvinced.

"Why don't you go back to the cabin and take a little rest before dinner?" Connie suggested. "This has been a busy few days. Maybe some rest will help you clear your head."

Caitlyn nodded and started for the door.

"And Caitlyn?" The girl paused. "It will work out. You and Mitchie will be okay. I promise."

Caitlyn smiled weakly. "I hope so," she

said. Then, turning once again, she left.

When she was alone, Connie let out another big sigh. She was going to have to have a little talk with Mitchie.

Colby had been right. Mr. Miller had been on his way to Camp Rock, and he had just arrived. Catching up to him on the path, Mitchie and Colby rushed into the parking lot. They came to an abrupt stop when they saw Mr. Miller's truck.

Mr. Miller looked like an older version of Colby. He had the same dark, intense eyes and wavy hair. He was sitting in the driver's seat, reading a sailing magazine. Hearing their footsteps, he looked up, grunted in acknowledgement, and went back to his article.

"Yikes," Mitchie said. "Not exactly the warm-and-fuzzy type, is he?"

A vein in Colby's forehead pulsed. He still couldn't believe his dad was here. Just another few hours and the competition would have been over. "I guess this is it," he said, defeated. "Mitchie—I, uh, I can't thank you enough."

"No!" Mitchie gulped. After she had alienated Caitlyn—and Shane—and made a fool of herself in a silly costume, Colby was *still* leaving. Fighting back tears, she turned and saw a figure striding through the woods. It was her mom.

"Oh, no," she said, more to herself than to Colby. "Was I supposed to be in the kitchen?"

She ran over. "I'm sorry, Mom," she began. "I didn't think I had kitchen duty, and it's just that . . ." Her voice trailed off as she saw the stern look on her mother's face.

"Mitchie, we have to talk," she said in a serious tone.

"Can we do it later?" She looked over her shoulder. Colby was still standing there, his expression hopeless.

Connie shook her head. "No, Mitchie."

There was no arguing. Sighing, Mitchie turned to Colby. "I promise I'll come find you just as soon as I can," she called. "Don't leave . . . not yet!"

Across camp, completely unaware of the drama, Tess and Lorraine were in the midst of a final dress-fitting. The two girls had spent hours poring over the trunks of costumes until Tess found one she thought was just right for the video. It was a deep, cobalt blue that brought out her eyes. Around the trim, there were beads that swung with every step she took and satin piping that gleamed when the light hit it. It looked like something a professional dancer would wear, and Tess was ecstatic. Now, she was standing on a stool as Lorraine made last-minute adjustments. On the bunks nearby, Ella and Peggy sat watching. They had to admit, at the moment, Tess looked every part the pop-star diva.

"Ella," Tess called over her shoulder. "Do

you have that cherry lip gloss your mom sent? I think that would go perfectly."

From her bunk, Ella nodded. Reaching over, she grabbed a giant makeup bag from off her bedside table. Rummaging around the dozens of lip glosses, she found the one Tess wanted. Pulling it out, she handed it to Tess. "It's totally perfect," Ella agreed.

Peggy frowned. She was all about her group winning this jam, but Tess seemed to be going overboard—again. The video was already almost entirely about her and Shane. And now, with her fabulous dress, no one would be looking anywhere else. After Final Jam, she thought for sure things would be different, that she wouldn't always be just outside the spotlight. But it seemed she was wrong.

As if reading her thoughts, Tess smiled confidently. "We are *so* going to win this competition," she said. "When everyone sees Shane and I on the big screen, they'll know that this is just the first step to my stardom. And I totally know that Gillian—who happens to be a good friend of my mother's—will let her know how great I was in the video. By this time next summer, I could be doing my very own number in one of her shows."

Looking up, Lorraine paused in midstitch. "Do you really think that you'll get to perform with your mom?" she asked in awe.

"Of course," Tess said, nodding. "True, everyone is all about how great Shane and Mitchie looked at Final Jam. But come on, this industry is all about star quality. And I don't know . . . I just don't think Mitchie's got it." What she didn't say was that she was actually very sure Mitchie *did* have it. But it wouldn't do Tess any good to voice her fears. She needed to prove to her mom, to everyone, that she was a star in the making. This video was going to do that—she was sure of it.

"Done," Lorraine said, standing up.

"You are one-hundred-percent fitted!"

Tess turned to look in the mirror and smiled. She had to hand it to Lorraine, the girl was good with costumes. Twirling one way and then another, Tess beamed. In a few short hours, their video would be complete and the results would be in—she just hoped that she got a first-place blue ribbon to go with her blue dress.

Looking back at Lorraine, she nodded approvingly. "Good. Now, let's discuss what I'll wear to the video viewing. When we win, I want to look red-carpet ready."

Peggy and Ella rolled their eyes. The next few hours were going to be *very* interesting.

CHAPTER THIRTEEN

Having left Colby to talk with his dad, Mitchie now walked silently toward the kitchen. In front of her, her mother's steps were steady and, Mitchie imagined, angry. But she didn't know what she had done wrong.

When they got to the kitchen, Connie leaned against an island. Mitchie stood across from her and waited.

"Caitlyn was in here earlier," her mom began. "She was very upset, Mitchie. She feels like you haven't been around much for her."

"It's not my fault," Mitchie said, immediately on the defensive. "She's been busy, too. And I've had a lot on my mind. First there was the whole Gillian thing and then the video—which is totally not working now, so we'll never win. . . ."

"You can't win everything," Connie said gently. "You know that. You didn't win Final Jam, but did that make it less special? Why is it so important you win *this*?"

Mitchie took a deep breath. She had to tell her mom what was going on. It was the right thing to do—even if it meant breaking her word.

Before she could change her mind, Mitchie began to talk. She told her mom about seeing Colby that first day. Then she told her about Colby's dad and how he would rather his son be miserable making boats than happy making music. As Mitchie spoke, Connie's expression softened.

When Mitchie finally finished, her mom pulled her into a hug. "Oh, Mitchie," she said gently. "That *is* a lot. But even though you want to help Colby, you have to figure out a way to balance that with your other friends. It's part of growing up."

"But . . ." Mitchie frowned.

"No buts."

Mitchie shrugged helplessly. Her mom was right. "I promised Colby I wouldn't let him down. If he has to go back home . . ."

"But you also promised Caitlyn you'd work with her on her music," she told her daughter.

"I know. *And* I promised Shane I'd listen to the song he did with Peggy, and I didn't do that either. I guess I was just trying to make everyone happy," Mitchie said glumly. "And I ended up making no one happy." She looked at her mother helplessly. "So what do I do?

Everyone's mad at me, and we only have a few hours left to make the video."

Connie smiled. "That's simple. I would start with the apologies," she said. "One thing I have discovered from being a wife and mother is that it doesn't take a long time to say 'I'm sorry.'"

Mitchie laughed. She could always count on her mother to give her good advice. "I'm sorry I've been so busy. Really sorry."

"See how easy that was?" her mom asked teasingly.

Mitchie grinned. "One down, three to go," she said. "Oh, and I'm going to take some cookies with me. They can only help."

Mitchie went to find Caitlyn first. She was sitting in their cabin, staring blankly at her laptop's screen saver.

"Hi," Mitchie said gently. She offered Caitlyn a cookie.

"No, thanks," Caitlyn said. "I've already

had like four hundred of those since yesterday."

Mitchie took a deep breath. "Listen, uh, I'm sorry," Mitchie began. Caitlyn sat up straighter. "I shouldn't have disappeared on you. You are a great friend—*the best*. And you didn't deserve me flaking out." Mitchie paused and took another deep breath. When Caitlyn didn't say anything, she went on. "I was wrapped up in helping out Colby." Mitchie decided to tell Caitlyn the truth about what was going on with Colby. When she was finished, she added, "That doesn't mean that Colby's replaced you as my BFF. No one could ever replace you."

Caitlyn smiled. "Do you really mean that?"

Mitchie returned the smile and nodded. "So, can we have a cookie and say we're friends again? Please?"

When Caitlyn took the cookie, Mitchie felt a weight lift off her shoulders. Things were already looking up.

Mitchie's apology mission wasn't over yet. Leaving her cabin, she headed toward Brown's, hoping to find Shane. Sure enough, she heard music coming from inside. The voice sounded like Shane's, but she'd never heard the song before. A girl's voice joined his. It was Peggy, Mitchie realized. Forgetting that she was even there to apologize, Mitchie dashed up to the cabin and knocked on the door. "Shane?" she called. "Is that the song? It's amazing!"

Shane came out onto the cabin porch, his hands stuffed into his pockets. He nodded. "I'm surprised you could make time to hear it."

His words stung. It had been hard saying she was sorry to Caitlyn, but this was going to be even harder. "Shane, you probably have every right to be mad at me. . . ."

Shane held up a hand, stopping her in

mid-sentence. "It's not entirely your fault," he said. "I wasn't exactly cool the past few days. And the funny thing is, I just wanted to talk to you. That was the whole point of me asking you to listen to the song. I've realized how much your opinion matters—and I thought you should know that."

Mitchie broke into a wide grin. He wasn't mad after all! But her smile faded when she noticed that Shane still looked upset.

"I think I owe Colby an apology, too," he said, his voice heavy.

Suddenly, Mitchie had an idea. . . .

Colby was leaving his cabin, his duffel bag slung over his shoulder, when Shane and Mitchie walked up.

After Mitchie had left, Colby's dad had informed him he had an hour to pack and get back to the truck—no ifs, ands, or buts. Time was up. Now, seeing Shane, Colby's eyes grew wide. "What brings you to my cabin? Or should I say, soon-to-be-ex–cabin. I mean, it doesn't have much star quality."

Shane knew he deserved that. "Hey, man. You're right. I was out of line. You deserve to be here as much as anyone."

Colby's mouth dropped open in surprise. "Wow. Uh, thanks."

"Don't thank me yet. I said you deserve to be here, but now we have to convince your dad. Mitchie filled me in. I hope you don't mind." He smiled. "Do you think he's ever heard of Connect Three?"

Colby jumped up in the air and let out a whoop. Shane Gray—*the* Shane Gray—was going to talk to his dad. Out of the corner of his eye, Colby saw his father step out of the truck. "That is awesome. You rock!"

"It's the least I can do," Shane said. "I've been trying to put my jerk behavior behind me."

Colby shook his head. "No," he said. "A jerk is someone who can't admit they're wrong. It's like what Nate said when we started the video—Camp Rock is all about stepping out of your comfort zone. Trying things again and again until you get them right. You definitely did that in coming over here, and that's awesome." Then, to Mitchie's amazement, Colby threw his bag on the ground. "Now it's time for me to try this again. It's time for me to stand up to my dad and tell him I deserve to be here. That's not your job, Shane."

Turning, Colby walked toward his dad, his head high.

Mitchie watched him go, an anxious expression on her face. "I wish you'd seen him the first day," she said to Shane. "He was so scared and unwilling to stand up for himself . . ." Suddenly, her eyes twinkled. "Shane! I think I just came up with a concept for the video." She looked at her watch. There wasn't much time.

"Well, what are you waiting for?" Shane

asked. "Go!" he exclaimed. "Go!"

She didn't need to be told twice. She started to run but stopped herself and turned around. "I swear we'll talk later. I don't mean to just take off like . . ."

He laughed. "Just go! And good luck!"

Mitchie took off down the path, her mind racing. They only had a short time to get this idea together, but if they could, Colby's dad would see something fantastic, and maybe, just maybe, Colby would get to stay.

She let out a squeak when she ran into Sander. "Sorry," she said, gasping for air. "I was looking for you. I have an idea!"

CHAPTER FOURTEEN

A few hours later, the videos were completed and both groups had gathered in the mess hall. Mitchie was sitting next to Caitlyn, her eyes scanning the crowd. She hadn't seen Colby since they wrapped the new video. He had convinced his father to let him stay through the final filming and end of the evening. But after that, if Mr. Miller wasn't impressed, Colby was leaving.

"Are you going to get in trouble for consorting with the enemy?" Caitlyn asked, interrupting her thoughts.

"You're only the enemy if you win," Mitchie said, smiling. "And we'll just see about that."

Her grin widened as she saw Colby and his dad walk into the mess hall. Colby caught her eye and nodded his head. They sat down just as Brown walked to the front of the room. A microphone was set up in front of a large screen.

"Hey, Camp Rock!" Brown shouted. He was met with a chorus of cheers. "I think we all agree this is a special place. And both these videos reflect the incredible talent that we have here. Before we begin, Gillian would like to say a few words."

Gillian stepped forward to take the mike. "Thank you, Brown," Gillian said. One of her dogs ran out to join her onstage, and she scooped it up in her arms.

The campers waited nervously.

"Let me just say these videos turned

out great. Better than I could ever have expected." There was a round of excited applause, and then she continued. "You're all going to be big stars. Unfortunately, only one team can be the winner tonight. So, without further adieu, the videos."

As the lights went down, Mitchie reached over and squeezed Caitlyn's hand. This was it.

Shane's team was first, and the audience was on their feet in seconds, clapping and cheering along as the music filled the room. The song was upbeat and lively. On the screen, Tess and Shane looked great. "He spins her around like she's made out of air," Mitchie said in awe. "And look how great her dress is! Where'd she find that in the middle of the woods?"

"I heard Lorraine helped her out. Looks like Tess not only got a new entourage member, she got a seamstress, too," Caitlyn commented.

Mitchie punched her gently on the arm. "Be nice," she said, smiling.

When the video ended, Shane's team stood up to take a bow. Tess and Lorraine had found another great outfit for the evening. Tess was wearing a yellow sundress and sparkly earrings. As everyone cheered, she took several more bows. Shane had to pull her into her seat to make her stop.

"Now ours!" Mitchie said, tapping her foot nervously.

The video was much different from Shane's. It didn't have the fast beat or wild dancing of the first one. Mitchie's and Colby's voices sang over the scenes. There was Colby, guitar in his hand, slumped in defeat beside his father's truck. Then he was standing tall and proud, full of confidence. This action was intercut skillfully with candid moments of campers: Mitchie and Lorraine kneading bread in the kitchen and messing up, Sander missing a beat on the drums, Lola and Ella trying on garish lip gloss. Then there were more shots of the groups fixing their mistakes and talking things out. The message was clear: fear is part of life, and no matter what you want to be and what your problems are, your friends will be there to pull you through.

When the video ended, the audience went wild.

Mitchie was beaming as the lights came on. They had done it! They had made an awesome video. No matter the outcome, they had given their all. And Colby might not get to stay, but he'd done his best and shown his dad what he could do. Looking over, she saw that Colby and his dad were leaving. Mitchie sprang up and raced over. "Don't you want to at least wait and find out who won?"

Mr. Miller turned and, for the first time since Mitchie had seen him, smiled. "I'm going," he said. "He's staying. I don't need to see who won to know my kid's got talent that shouldn't be wasted. You did good, kiddo." Pulling Colby into a hug, he clapped him on the back twice, then nodded and left.

For a moment, neither Mitchie nor Colby said anything. "Wow," Colby said when he found his voice. "This day didn't turn out the way I thought it would."

"That's what makes camp . . ." Mitchie started to say. But she was interrupted by the sound of Brown tapping on the microphone. Everyone grew quiet. This was the moment.

"It was a hard decision," Brown said. "But in the end, we decided the winner is . . . 'Swing Time'!"

Around her, Mitchie heard people clapping and shouting for Shane's team. She smiled. Colby was right. The day hadn't ended the way she imagined either. It had turned out *better*. She went to join Caitlyn, Shane, Colby, and the rest of the campers.

She had the rest of the summer to win a competition. Now, she just wanted to enjoy the only prize that mattered—her friends.

DISNEP

CAMP ROCK

SECOND
SESSION
#2

For The Record

By Lucy Ruggles

Based on "Camp Rock," Written by Karin Gist & Regina Hicks and Julie Brown & Paul Brown

"Now for the secret ingredient," Mitchie Torres said triumphantly as she dumped a bag of confectioners' sugar into the jumbo bowl in front of her. Some of the white powder wafted back into the air and settled on her head, making her brown hair appear streaked with gray.

But Mitchie didn't care. She was helping her mother, Connie Torres, bake up a batch of brownies, and she was in a good mood—a fabulous mood, actually. And why shouldn't she be? The sun was shining, the campers were singing, the familiar faces were all there (plus a few new ones), and it was another beautiful morning at Camp Rock.

"That makes three of us in the entire world who know the secret ingredient to Connie's Baritone Brownies," Mitchie said, brushing sugar from her hands and smiling at her mother. "You, me, and now Caitlyn."

"Just three?" Connie asked as she placed the spinning blades of a mixer into the chocolate batter. A smile crossed her face. "You mean you haven't told Shane?"

Mitchie's friend and cabinmate, Caitlyn Gellar, was standing next to her at the kitchen counter. She laughed as her friend's face turned bright red.

Caitlyn's days of working in the kitchen as punishment for last session's food fight with Tess Tyler were over, but she still liked to hang out with Mitchie and Connie. Sometimes she even brought her laptop along to let them preview her latest musical creation.

"Is that what you think of me?" Mitchie asked, playing along with her mom. "That I'd reveal something as top secret as your brownie recipe to the first pop star to become my friend?"

True, Mitchie and Shane Gray had shared a fantastic moment the night of Final Jam when they had sung together in front of everyone. But even though she wanted to tell him about silly things like her mom's brownie recipe, there just wasn't enough time! Now that Camp Rock's Second Session was in full swing, her days were packed with jams, classes, singing, and dancing with all her new friends.

Still, she thought, Shane Gray! I can't believe I'm friends with one of the members of Connect Three—one of the biggest bands ever! It feels like a dream. . . .

Connie laughed, breaking into Mitchie's reverie. "I'm afraid there are more than three in the brownie 'know.' I told your father."

"Mrs. Torres!" Caitlyn exclaimed. "Loose lips sink ships!"

Their conversation was interrupted by the entrance of Camp Rock's director, Brown Cesario.

"Hello, masters of the Mess Hall of Fame," Brown said as he came into the kitchen.

"Don't you mean *mistresses* of the Mess Hall of Fame?" corrected Mitchie.

Brown nodded. "Of course," he agreed. "Ooh, brownies!" He dipped his finger into the rich, fudgy batter.

Connie swatted him away. "Brown, keep

your hands out of my Baritone Brownies," she chided.

"Named after me, I'm sure." He winked. "Sorry. Can't help myself. This day just keeps getting better and better."

"Why's that?" Caitlyn asked.

Brown looked thoughtful, as if weighing whether or not he should tell them. But he quickly cracked. "I just heard that my old friend Rex Riley is dropping in tomorrow for a surprise visit."

Caitlyn's eyes nearly popped out of her head. "You mean, *Rex Riley*?" she asked, astonished.

Brown nodded. "That's the one. I haven't seen him much since I was touring with Guns N' Roses—they were opening for Aerosmith—and he was just getting started, doing some promotion for INXS," he said wistfully. For a moment he gazed off into space, as if remembering something from long, long ago.

Caitlyn was speechless. "Wow," she finally managed to say.

But Connie and Mitchie just looked at each other in confusion. Neither of them had any clue who Rex Riley was or why his visit would cause the normally chatty Caitlyn to be rendered mute. But it looked like they were about to find out.